Ben Alexander and His Magic Farts

Written and illustrated by

Debbie A. Smith

ISBN-13: 979-8-46416-395-9

Ben Alexander and His Magic Farts

For Ben, my inspiration,
with love from Granny Apple

This book belongs to:

_____

Contents

Chapter 1, The Call to Help

Doofus, the dragon, was being beaten. His best friend, and oft-time challenger, Dod, the unicorn, was once again beating him. At last count, this was the forty-third time that Dod had beaten him. "Oh no," sighed Doofus, as he resignedly pushed away his playing cards and slumped back in his chair, making it creak and wobble alarmingly. The chair tipped back and crashed noisily into the castle wall behind it. "Not again!" he said, as he righted the chair and pulled it back from the wall. "I'm never going to win!"

Dod smiled and gathered the playing cards into a neat pile ready for putting back into their box, along with the cribbage board and its matchsticks. "Don't worry Doofus," she said, "It's only a game and you are improving. You were only sixteen behind me this time you know." She tossed her mane away from her face and frowned. It did irritate her the way her mane insisted on falling over her eyes, she really would need to make a hairdresser's appointment one of these days. She reached across and soothingly patted Doofus on his green and purple outstretched arm as he started to lever himself out of his somewhat undersized armchair.

Doofus sighed again. "I know," he said. "I think it's more that I'm bored. It's been ages since we were needed. I know that's good, because it means that the children are all well and happy without us. I'm so glad that we have been given this wonderful job of using our skills to help make problems go away, but it's always so much better when we are busy and helping, rather than just sitting around here and waiting like this."

Dod started to respond with some soothing words when suddenly the magic horn on her head, the famous magic unicorn's horn, erupted into flashes of pulsating vibrant rainbow colours. "Your wish is apparently answered Doofus!" she giggled.

Doofus jumped up in surprised delight, knocking over the table and sending playing cards and cribbage board flying across the tartan carpeted floor. His glossy coat of shiny mail started to similarly pulsate and shimmer with glistening hues of purple and green, as if in time with Dod's flashing horn.

"Yippee!" he cried, as he rather clumsily danced around the room in excitement, knocking books from the bookcase and making Tavi, the Scottie dog, who had been happily sleeping in front of the fire, growl in disgust as she lost the trail of the wonderful bone she had been dreaming about. "Who is needing us this time Dod?"

Dod carefully stepped over the fallen books and trotted to the white wall at the back of the room, always kept clean and spotless for such times, and directed her flashing horn to the white space which seemed to glow back at them in happy expectation.

A message started to take shape on the wall before them. "Ben Alexander needs your help urgently," the message read.

Chapter 2, Ben meets Doofus and Dod

Back in Fortrose, in the Highlands of Scotland, Ben Alexander hid under his duvet and tried to stop the tears that threatened to spill from his tightly closed eyes. "It wasn't fair," he thought miserably, "my farts used to make people laugh." He and Dad used to have so much fun playing farting competitions while play fighting on the living room floor. However, Ben's farts were just not the same these days. He hated them, he decided. It had frightened him a bit last week when that little fart had squeezed out, despite him trying to hold it in, when he was in Helen's kitchen. It was such a little fart, and he didn't think it had smelt all that bad, but Helen had bumped her head when she fainted after smelling it and Mum had given him such a row and marched him straight back home after checking that Helen was fine and fully recovered. Now it had happened again and this time with a worse outcome.

He lay in bed and listened as the ambulance drove away with the poor delivery man who had been caught unawares, as Ben had accidentally let another fart slip, as he had reached to take the parcel from the delivery man at the front door. The ambulance man had assured Mum that the delivery man would be okay, and his ankle, would feel fine once it had a proper stookie put on it, but he had then added, "It was strange that the delivery man had fallen so awkwardly whist simply trying to give your son a parcel wasn't it?" The ambulance man had looked over to Ben as he said this, and Ben hadn't liked the rather nervous and confused expression on the man's face as he had turned away from Ben.

He heard raised voices from downstairs and tried to cover his ears so that he wouldn't hear his parents arguing. "It's me they are fighting about," he thought miserably. "Everything is going wrong and it's all my fault." He tried to remember what Mum had said to him about being brave and positive and not imagining that he was to blame every time when things sometimes went wrong around him. He swallowed hard and tried to take a deep breath. Mum had said that doing that would help when he got upset. The breath was interrupted by a hiccup, and even a deep breath felt impossible. He started to cry in earnest, until a sudden whooshing sound, accompanied by a bright flash, startled him into shocked silence. Nervously, he slowly pulled the bed covers away from his face and peeked out. He couldn't believe his eyes! Right there, in front of him, were two of the most incredible creatures who looked like they must have jumped right out of one of his many books! Too shocked to even make a sound, Ben just looked at them open mouthed in amazement. His fuddled brain tried to take in and explain all that he saw. Standing there, in his very own bedroom, were a dragon and a unicorn! The dragon was the biggest, bigger than Dad; so big that it was nearly touching the ceiling! It seemed to glitter both purple and green and was covered in little spiky bits, a bit like fish scales. It seemed to have an impressive tail too, but he couldn't see much of it properly as the dragon was sitting on most of it. The unicorn was smaller and her

slightly furry coat looked like a moving

rainbow in a funny sort of way. It had a

very impressive golden tail and a mane,

also in gold, flowing down its neck and

over its face. But the most impressive

thing about the unicorn was the large

shining horn that stuck up from its head. It

was stunning; Ben couldn't take his eyes

off it. He didn't think he had ever seen such an enthralling sight in his life

before. He was completely fascinated. It seemed to make him feel calm

and dreamy in a very reassuring and comforting sort of way. As Ben lay

there, enjoying this wonderfully lovely feeling, he noticed that both

creatures were smiling at him. No, not just smiling, they were grinning

broadly at him.

"Hello Ben," said the unicorn. "My name is Dod and I'm so pleased to

meet you."

"And my name is Doofus," said the dragon, as he beamed the most enormous grin and then he slowly put out a giant paw as if to shake Ben's hand.

Ben fleetingly wondered why this all did now feel so completely fine and normal, before happily dismissing the thought. This just felt very right, and very safe, and he actually even felt like these lovely creatures were almost a part of him in some sort of magical and wonderful way. He enthusiastically threw the duvet back and jumped out of bed to meet the outstretched paw with his own hand. It wasn't just a handshake, like you would get when you first met someone new, like your first teacher, or someone like that though, this felt like a magically huge, fantastic hug. It made him sigh with relief and delight, like all the troubles and worries he had ever

had just floated away into nothingness.

"We hear that you've been having some farting troubles, Ben. We are here to help and make things better," said Dod. The dragon, Doofus, was staring admiringly around Ben's room. "I love your bedroom," he said. He was looking at Ben's toy tools and the stand that his grandparents had given him for Christmas some years ago, when Ben was small. "I wish I had a set like this," Doofus went on to say. "You could build so much with these." His face took on a faraway look, "Maybe I could build myself a new workshop in the castle tower with these…"

Doofus was interrupted in his musings by a sharp "Harrumph" and over exaggerated clearing of her throat by Dod. She tossed her mane and Ben was momentarily mesmerised by the fine shower of golden dust that flew as she shook her head. Dod looked vaguely irritated for a second and Ben heard her mutter "I really do need that hairdresser appointment," before she looked apologetically at him. "I'm sorry about that dust, I will get it hoovered up later I promise," she said, before turning sharply to Doofus. "No time for playing with tools just now Doofus," she said firmly. Doofus reluctantly, but obediently, dropped the toy pliers he had been holding back into the toolbox and shuffled back over to stand beside her again.

"Oh, please don't worry about the dust," Ben said quickly. "It's beautiful, and my Mum loves hoovering anyway." He turned to Doofus. "The tools are only pretend you know. You can't make anything real with them." He started to say more but was abruptly interrupted by Dod. "I hope you are not saying that hoovering is only a job for Mums young man?" she said sternly. Her horn seemed to be suddenly glowing with a darker colour. "Housework is boring but necessary and everyone, no matter who or what they are, needs to share the chores involved." She paused, clearly waiting for an appropriate response from Ben. He shuffled from one foot to the other in embarrassment and tried to cover the passing surprise, and perhaps a little guilt that he had felt as she said her stern words. "I do try to help quite a lot, but…"

"No buts Ben and no excuses. Make sure you do help out where you can in future. Anyway, enough of that," she smiled reassuringly again, and her horn glowed anew, now returned to the rainbow hues of earlier. Ben, relieved to see her smile, returned her smile and nodded his head vigorously. He was about to say more but stopped as Dod tutted loudly whilst glaring over at Doofus. Relieved that the Unicorn's apparent irritation was no longer directed at him, Ben turned to see what was annoying her now. Maybe he wasn't the only one who got things wrong sometimes.

Doofus was still looking across longingly at Ben's tool set. "In your world they may be pretend tools" he began to explain, "but in my world, pretend things can become real, especially if they are useful like these are. Oh, I can see such a good design for my workshop. The desk would be the size of..."

"Doofus remember what we are here for please?" implored Dod, with a touch of impatience, although she did smile to show that she wasn't really that cross. "Ben doesn't want to listen to your plans just now."

"Actually," retorted Ben, "I really do. Your world sounds great. What..."

Before he could even finish his question, he had to stifle a giggle as Doofus gathered himself up, clearly excited about the opportunity to share his ideas with someone who sounded genuinely interested. Before his explanation was begun, however, he was halted by a look from Dod.

Looking a tad embarrassed, he responded, shrugging his shoulders, and glancing ruefully in Dod's direction. "Umm, yes, well, maybe some other time." He looked back at Ben and made a dramatic, if somewhat stunted bow to him. There really was so little spare room in the bedroom with such magical creatures squeezed in as well. Ben was impressed with how Doofus had managed to even make such a move. He then rather grandly announced, "**You** are the important one here just now." He tried to finish the bow with a flourish, but nearly tripped over his tail and was only stopped from a very clumsy fall by Dod's speedy reactions. He did, however, still clatter into the wardrobe doors which made them rattle noisily and alarmingly and even the wall seemed to wobble a bit.

Ben was more than a little taken aback. "I'm important? You're here for me? I don't understand?" As he said these words, it crossed Ben's mind that it really wasn't normal to have a real-life dragon and a real-life unicorn standing in the middle of his bedroom and why hadn't anyone downstairs come up to see what on earth the noise and goings on upstairs was all about anyway?

Again, Doofus seemed to know Ben's thoughts. His eyes twinkled. "It is funny isn't it? Who would have thought that such a thing could really happen? No-one else is aware of what is happening here just now Ben," he explained gently. "And sorry about your wardrobe doors, but don't worry about them. I can easily repair them if I have to. I love repairing things, almost as much as I like making things really. It's actually hard to say which is more fun….?" He stopped abruptly as he saw the expression on Dod's face, and then quickly continued. "Don't worry about your Mum and Dad, or even your sister, although she would probably be more aware and be coming to see what was going on if she was here, instead of being at nursery just now. Your Mum and Dad, though, won't be worried at all. We make time different you see. It's complicated, but time is sort of frozen for them just now, but it will all go back to normal once we are finished with helping you out." Doofus looked over to Dod who, after a dramatic shake of her mane, that Ben rightly assumed was done in irritation at Doofus, then turned back to face Ben and continued. "I understand," she asked, "that you've been having troubles with your farts recently?" Ben looked down, embarrassed and a bit confused. "How could they possibly know about

17

that?" he thought. "He hadn't spoken about his farts to anyone, not even Mum."

Again, appearing to read Ben's thoughts, Doofus interrupted. "Don't be embarrassed. This is none of your doing Ben. We know what's been happening and, even better, we know why your farts are causing these problems and we can sort it for you." This last statement was made with such obvious pride and delight that Ben couldn't help but giggle. He already felt so much better.

"Can you remember when you first noticed anything was strange Ben?" asked Dod. "Err, I'm not sure I understand?" mumbled Ben, feeling distracted and confused. "What do you mean by strange?"

Doofus looked questionably at Dod. "Perhaps I might be able to explain this one better Dod?" Once again, her mane was shaken, and she tutted anew as more golden dust fell to the floor. She sighed resignedly, nodded encouragingly, and even stepped back and sat on her haunches to let Doofus continue. Doofus smiled back in thanks. "Ben," he began, "Why don't you get yourself comfortable on your bed and I'll try to explain it to you." Ben dutifully drew his duvet up from the floor where it had fallen and curled it up around him into a comfy cushion shape,

settled down and then looked expectantly at Doofus.

Chapter 3, The Magic of Magic!

"Sometimes bits of magic escape from our world," Doofus started to explain, but paused when he noticed Ben suddenly starting to look anxious. "No, no," he reassured, "Nothing too bad." Dod appeared to cough suddenly beside him. He glanced quickly over to her and they exchanged looks in what seemed to be a meaningful way. Doofus continued, clearly taking more time to consider his words. "The magic is very rarely bad, but even when it sometimes appears to be bad, it's usually because it's not good at understanding how things are in this world. It's not good at explaining its intentions, and then it gets cross because people in this world don't understand what the magic is saying or trying to do. This makes it then do naughty things in frustration. The magic is not supposed to come across to your world. However, when the magic is still young and not yet fully grown, it may be dared by other young magic. It may mistakenly think it's being very brave and clever and then makes the mistake of ignoring the rules and jumping over here to have some fun."

Doofus paused and looked at Ben more closely for a second. "I'm sure you can think of some of your friends at school who have dared you, or others, to do silly things sometimes?" Ben thought a moment. "Yes," he responded thoughtfully. "There was that time when a boy in the class above him had dared him to stand up on the bus and shout that Miss Davidson, who was his teacher and who Ben actually really liked, was a big poo." Ben reddened and felt a bit horrified at what he had just thought as he suddenly remembered that Doofus would know his thoughts. He hung his head and waited for a reaction, expecting to be given a row. After a moment of silence, he dared to look up and found both of them smiling at him. "You were lucky," said Doofus. "You managed to be strong enough to not take up that dare." Doofus winked at him. "It was close though Ben wasn't it? You nearly were drawn into doing it weren't you?" Ben nodded rather sheepishly, and Doofus patted him on his shoulder reassuringly. Doofus continued. "Well, the magic is a bit like that. It's hard for them to resist dares sometimes, especially when they want to make friends and impress other more experienced magic. However, once the magic enters your world, it doesn't take long before it realises that it's not so clever or so brave, and that there's no-one around to see and be impressed, or to help them. Then it starts to get people into trouble as it's revenge. Left long enough, the magic usually grows up a bit and works out how to get itself back to our world without too many problems being caused but, unfortunately, it sometimes can leave a bit of a mess behind."

"What sort of a mess?" asked Ben a little nervously. Again, a look passed meaningfully between Doofus and Dod. "Well," pondered Doofus, "you remember that time when the swing park up the road was vandalised, and the swings were left broken, and some horrible things were scrawled on various places around the village?" Ben nodded, and then leaned forward excitedly. "Was that the magic that did that?" he asked incredulously. "In a way it was." replied Doofus. Seeing Ben's confused expression, he explained further. "It WAS a couple of young people who did it, but the thoughts to do so were put in their minds by the magic. Sometimes the magic finds it easier when the young people are already feeling similar to the magic. If they are already feeling resentful about what they are not allowed to do and angry enough then, in partnership with the magic, they can carry out some pretty horrible activities. Both the magic, and the young people that do these things, think that it will make them feel better, but it rarely, if ever, does." Some of this explanation seemed hard to understand for Ben but seeing the upset expressions on Doofus's and Dod's faces, he realised that this was both serious and worrying. He sat and considered for a moment, and then looked at them both, his face registering both fear and horror. "But what has all this to do with me and my farts?"

Both Doofus and Dod jumped in surprise as Ben spoke. They had both got lost in their own thoughts and appeared to have forgotten his presence momentarily.

This time it was Dod who replied. "Oh, I'm so sorry Ben, it's so easy to get side-tracked when thinking about such happenings." She bent forward and blew gently on his face which tickled and made him giggle. "You are a completely different story. Your magic is unusual, but easier to deal with." Ben shook his head a little, getting more puzzled by the second. Before he had chance to comment, Dod continued. "The magic tends to go towards people who are of a similar age stage to themselves, so your magic influence isn't one of the more difficult to deal with, unlike the magic that has more teenage-like effects. Your magic is younger and mischievous but would really be happier if it was helped back to its own world. It is unusual for younger magic to escape from our world. It must have been clever magic, and it obviously was looking for someone about its own age and just as clever," Dod stopped and smiled at Ben. "Someone just like you it seems." Ben blushed, chuffed, but a bit embarrassed. "It sounds like it just got a bit stuck in this world, so then it started making more obvious mischief as a way of asking for help." Dod paused and searched Ben's face to check that he was following what she was saying. Apparently satisfied with his smile in response, she continued. "Now, we need to work out when and how the magic managed to get to your fart centre first."

"What do you mean my 'fart centre'?" laughed Ben. His mind already imagining funny pictures of such a thing whizzing around inside his tummy. This time it was Doofus's turn to look puzzled. "Surely you know about your fart centre?" he asked. Ben looked blankly back at him.

"Everyone starts off with a fart centre when they are born," explained Doofus. "Evidence shows that the centres appear to be most active in boys, although they can remain strong even in fully adult men too, but everyone can have fun with them if they know how to use them properly. We have them, just the same, in our world and there are special teaching sessions in both nursery and school to help our children learn how to have the most fun with them. Didn't you go to your teaching sessions on these then?" Ben looked blankly at both Doofus and Dod. "I've never heard of such a thing," he said, "though I really like the sounds of that. What else do they do?" Doofus and Dod exchanged shocked expressions at each other. "Dod, this might help to explain some other recent happenings. We must pass this information on as soon as we get back home again." Dod nodded her head vigorously, sending a rich cloud of gold dust right up as far as the ceiling. So animated were they both, that neither seemed to notice the dust, even as Ben leant forward to catch the dust as it fell and felt it tickle and tingle as it slid through his fingers. He slipped his bare feet down to the carpet and enjoyed the sensation even more when it trickled through his toes.

"We will try to explain more at a later time to you Ben, but we really need to get on with sorting this out for you," said Dod. Ben felt a bit disappointed, he really did like the sounds of this amazing fart centre thing, but he sighed and nodded in agreement. "Was there any time, before your farts started to be troublesome, that you remember feeling a bit strange?" Ben looked a little bewildered. Dod tossed her mane back in slight irritation and looked to Doofus. He quickly responded after flashing her an understanding grin first. "Do you remember feeling any funny tingling feelings, like shivers, only much stronger and more tickly?" he asked.

Ben thought and thought. Suddenly his face lit up. "Yes, yes, I remember!" he cried, almost falling off his bed in his excitement to explain. "There was that day when we all went down to the beach and I went paddling with my wellies on. I went a bit too far into the sea and a wave came and splashed over into my wellies and filled them right up and soaked my trouser legs too." Ben also remembered Mum shouting at him to get back out of the sea and him feeling really cross with her for spoiling his fun too, but he didn't tell Doofus about that. "Ahh," said Doofus knowingly, and Ben realised that Doofus had already read his thoughts. Ben looked down, feeling a bit ashamed, but Doofus carried on, ignoring his reaction. "Did you empty your wellies of the water straight away?"

"No," replied Ben. "It tickled and felt funny and made me giggle and then it sort of tickled more all the way up my legs and into my tummy." He giggled at the memory. "Did you feel any shivers," asked Dod. She was so close to Ben now that he could feel her tickly breath again on his face, but he tried to concentrate hard again to remember. "Not right then I don't think, "he replied slowly, "but I do remember that after we walked back home then I couldn't stop shivering for ages, even after I had changed into warm dry clothes and had had a mug of hot drinking chocolate. I remember that I kept on nearly spilling my drink because my hands were shaking so much." He looked eagerly at them both to see if this was what they were hoping to hear. It was. Doofus clapped his giant paws together and beamed, clearly delighted. Ben glanced at Dod and gasped. Her horn was glowing really brightly and she too, was grinning broadly. "That's it! That's when it happened!" exclaimed Doofus. He reached across and pulled Ben's duvet back up onto the bed and

plumped it back into a cosy nest-like cushion. Ben clambered back onto

the bed and they waited whilst he got himself cosy and comfortable once

again. Ben's heart felt like it was beating so hard that it might burst out

of him. He was a bit nervous about what he was yet to hear, but it was

oh so exciting too! He just knew these two amazing creatures were the

best and that no matter whatever had happened to him, that these two

were going to be able to sort it all out for him too!

Chapter 4, Preparing to Fix the Farts.

"So, what happens now?" Ben asked eagerly. "How are you going to fix my farts?" he giggled. Even saying it sounded so silly. Imagine his farts being something that needed to be fixed! Doofus had clearly picked up on Ben's thoughts as he started to laugh too. Within seconds the two of them were helpless with laughter. Ben laughed so hard that he cried. Trying hard not to laugh herself, Dod interceded. "Come on you pair," she half gasped. "Get a grip! We've got work to do!"

Ben and Doofus both took deep breaths and fought to stop the waves of laughter that kept threatening to erupt again and again. Eventually, after a few minutes and a few "Harrumphs" and mane shakes from Dod, they succeeded, and both looked to Dod, waiting for her to detail their plan of action.

"Fixing the farts themselves is relatively easy," she advised, "but we have two options of how we may best do it. The main thing we need to do is to get you in a bath of warm water..." Ben fidgeted a bit, wondering how the solution could have anything to do with just having a bath. Dod continued on, ignoring the minor interruption, "...and we can either do that here in your house, but we would need to magic your family so they weren't aware, or we could take you to our home and get you in a bath there. Given our time difference, we could go and return you back without your Mum and Dad even being aware that you had been anywhere." Dod turned to look questioningly at Doofus. "What do you think Doofus?"

Before Doofus even had a chance to respond, Ben jumped up excitedly, "Oh please, PLEASE, can we go to your home?" he asked desperately. Such an adventure opportunity was just too important to miss, he was certain of that. He looked pleadingly from Dod to Doofus and back at Dod again. "PLEEEAASE?"

Dod and Doofus looked at each other, already smiling at Ben's eagerness. Doofus nodded agreeably at Dod. "Okay Ben, BUT..." Dod said firmly, as Ben started to jump up and down in excitement. She waited, with a stern expression on her face until Ben stopped and paid proper attention to her. "There are rules you have to follow if you are coming to our home." Ben nodded eagerly, before she could say anything more. "I will, I will," he said quickly. Doofus snorted a bit, trying to stop himself from laughing and gently pushed Ben back to get him to sit once more on his bed.

"Sit there a moment and listen carefully Ben, "he said. "These rules are important." Ben took in a deep breath and slowly let it out again. He sat up straight and looked, he hoped, attentively at them both. "Okay," he said, "I'm ready."

Dod smiled gratefully at him and began. "There really are only two main rules you have to follow," she said. "Rule One: You MUST do as we say and not, under any circumstances, go wandering off on your own." Ben nodded eagerly in agreement. Dod caught his eye and held his gaze for, what felt like, a very long moment. She looked quite stern and Ben swallowed uncomfortably. "It will be safe inside our castle, although even there, there are rooms and places you MUST NOT go unless one of us is with you. It would NOT be safe for you to go outside the castle at any time ever. Is that clear?" Ben nodded again, though he was beginning to feel a little scared. What was he letting himself in for? Should he maybe just stay here instead? "Rule Two…" Dod started to say, and then stopped and smiled at him, "You must eat this chocolate before we go." As she said this, she turned to Doofus, who put one of his big paws into, what looked like pouch on his tummy, similar to one like a kangaroo has for its baby. He pulled his paw out and held out a bar of chocolate for Ben, who eagerly reached for it. "One of my favourites," he gasped, recognising the brightly coloured wrapper. However, as he leant forward, Doofus pulled it quickly back out of his reach. "Hey, wait a minute first," Doofus said. "You need to know why

this chocolate is important. It's not just because you like it, you know."

"No," continued Dod. "The fact that you have chocolate at all is all down to us you know." Ben was stunned and looked at Dod in amazement.

"Whatever do you mean?" he said.

"Do you know that chocolate is made from cocoa beans which are grown on a plant?" asked Dod. Ben nodded. He thought he remembered Dad saying something about that a while ago, though he hadn't really paid much attention at the time as he had been too busy enjoying eating some chocolate.

"Well, we, that is some of the grown-up magic from our world, made the cocoa bean plant for your world to plant and then we helped your people to learn how to make chocolate from it." Ben stared at Dod open mouthed. "Really?" he squeaked. "Yes, really," retorted Dod. "You know, I'm sure, that chocolate makes you feel good, don't you?"

"Mmmn", agreed Ben, still puzzling about magic coming to his world to make sure people ate chocolate. "Well, we put magic into the cocoa beans to make people feel good. We hoped that it would help people be happy and kind to each other and stop them being upset and fighting each other."

"It makes me happy." said Ben, still eying up the chocolate bar. Doofus laughed. "In a minute, "he said, "but listen to Dod first please."

Ben grinned sheepishly and looked back at Dod.

Dod flicked her mane from her face and continued. "Yes, it works, but not maybe as much as we would have liked. People have since played around with different chocolate recipes and added things, which has somewhat reduced its power unfortunately. However, to come back to this chocolate bar…" She sighed as Ben again looked at the bar. "You may as well give him it Doofus, as I can see he's desperate for it," she said grudgingly. Doofus passed the bar to Ben who quickly unwrapped it. A muffled "fankyou", emerged from his smiling lips as he then began to eat the bar. "Well, we can certainly see it works here Dod", Doofus said laughingly.

"So it would appear," she replied, giving the tiniest flick of her mane. "This chocolate will also help you pass more easily into our world Ben. These particular kind of chocolate bars are particularly high in the magic essence and we can key in the code, now that you have eaten it, to let you come back with us to our castle. Will you please cover your feet with some of the golden dust lying on the floor from my mane please? I also need you to lift your jumper, so that I can see your tummy please. If you do that, I will get ready." She closed

her eyes as Ben quickly slid off his bed and wriggled his feet about in

the pile of tickly golden dust, whilst also fumbling to lift his jumper.

"No rush," said Doofus. "It will take Dod a minute or two to get the code

ready. You know," Doofus continued, "Your Mum really helped you by

giving you that hot chocolate drink after the magic got into you after your

seaside paddle." Ben stopped and stared at Doofus. "She did? How?"

he asked bluntly. "Does she know the magic stuff too then?"

"Not consciously I don't think," Doofus replied, "but, like lots of parents,

she knows that a bit of chocolate here and there makes you feel good,

and I think she instinctively knew that it would be of help to you, even if

she wasn't fully aware of why she needed to give you the chocolate."

"So more magic then?" suggested Ben smiling with delight at his Mum

doing a little bit of magic stuff too. Doofus nodded. "Yes, very probably.

There's lots even Dod and I don't know or understand about the power

of magic."

At that Dod opened eyes. "I'm ready," she said. Ben lifted up his jumper

so that she could see his bare tummy. Dod then knelt forward and pointed her horn, so that it almost, but not quite, touched his tummy."

The horn then started to pulse with vivid golden flashes of colour. "Ohh, that really tickles," Ben giggled and then he immediately fell asleep.

When he awoke, Ben was no longer in his bedroom.

Chapter 5, Meeting Tavi

 When Ben woke up, he found himself lying on a settee in a large, rather dark and grand room. Not a bad dark and grand room though. It felt almost as if the room itself was glad to see him too. Ben giggled. It did feel a bit strange, but in a nice way. The room was softly lit by lamps hanging from two of its walls and a log fire was brightly burning in the huge fireplace opposite him. He felt cosy and a little drowsy but realised that he had been awakened by a heavy weight pressing on his legs. He looked down, whilst trying to move his legs away from the weight, to be met by a very hairy, black doggie face. Its black eyes sparkled, and it

spoke. "At last, "it said, "I thought you would never wake up. Welcome to Magicarea."

Ben sat up in alarm, not quite believing his eyes and, more importantly, his ears. A talking dog? Impossible. "Did…," he took a deep breath and started again, "Did you just speak?" he said, not daring to believe there would be a response.

"Of course I did," replied the dog indignantly. "It would be very rude of me to ignore you now wouldn't it?" The dog stuck out a paw to Ben. "I'm Tavi. Pleased to meet you!" Tavi appeared to be a black Scottie dog, remarkably similar to the dog that his grandparents back home in Aberdeenshire owned, though that Tavi certainly didn't speak at all! Tavi was now sitting beside him on the settee, but Ben was pretty sure that the dog had been lying across his legs a minute ago. Stunned into silence, Ben gently shook the dog's paw. "That's better," said Tavi. The dog jumped off the settee and gave itself a shake. After sitting down and giving it's ear a quick scratch, Tavi turned and looked up at Ben, who hadn't moved at all, clearly still mesmerised by the dog. "Don't say much do you?" said Tavi, "I had hoped to have a bit more of a chat with you. I'm curious to know more about your world you know."

"Well," stammered Ben, "It's not every day you meet a talking dog you know."

Tavi jumped to her feet in apparent alarm. "What do you mean? Do you mean to tell me that you don't have talking dogs in your world?" The dog now looked as shocked as Ben had looked a minute or two earlier. "Well, no, we don't" Ben replied, now a little irritated at Tavi's scathing disbelief. "What a complete and utter waste of good intelligence that is then, I would say," she responded. She was clearly about to launch into a lengthier response when the door opened and in shuffled Doofus.

"I hope you are making our guest feel welcome and at home Tavi?" Doofus looked Ben over. "Ah," he continued, "Good to see you looking so good Ben. Dod sends her apologies. She thinks she slightly overdid it with the golden dust. She hadn't realised that the pile was as big as it was. You got a bit more magic than she had intended."

"Err, no worries," began Ben a little hesitantly, but was interrupted by Tavi. "Do you realise that they don't even listen to dogs speaking in his world?" she angrily snapped at Doofus. "Hey that's not quite right," responded Ben sharply. How dare this dog start criticising his world. Tavi and Ben glared at each other. "Hey, Hey," soothed Doofus. "Tavi behave, we've told you before that dogs don't have the same power in that world as you do in this world. Why are you giving Ben a hard time over this? It's not his fault and, more to the point, it's VERY rude of you to behave like this to him. He's a guest, and it must all be a bit frightening and strange to him." As he said this, Doofus looked at Ben, who looked a bit shamefaced and not at all frightened at all.

Tavi immediately put her head down, pattered to Ben's side, placed her head on his knee and looked up at him with such sad looking eyes, that Ben immediately forgot his anger and felt quite sorry for the little dog.

"I'm so sorry Ben," said Tavi in a miserable small voice. "Please forgive me. I know they had told me that things were different in your world, but I just didn't want to believe it. I behaved badly to you and I really do want to be your friend. Do you want me to go into the naughty corner as punishment? I will do so if it would make you feel better you know."

Tavi looked so concerned and so miserable that Ben felt like pulling her up onto his knee and giving her a huge cuddle. However, he was still a little nervous about the whole idea of a talking dog, so he held back a little but smiled and gently stroked the little dog. "It's ok Tavi, "he said soothingly. "I would like to be your friend too." Tavi's tail immediately started to wag and she jumped up, putting her paws on Ben's knees, so that she could reach his face. She gave him a huge lick, which tickled and made him laugh.

Doofus laughed at them both. "That's better both of you," he said.

"Where is Dod?" asked Ben, tickling Tavi's tummy as she lay on her back, clearly enjoying the experience, her tail thumping the thick tartan carpet as she furiously wagged it to and fro.

"She's at the hairdressers actually", said Doofus. "Her mane had become so thick that that was why she was having difficulty in managing the amount of golden dust it was making. She won't be too long but suggested we could give you a wee tour of the castle, if you would like, while we are waiting for her. How does that sound?"

Ben immediately stopped tickling Tavi, much to her clear

disappointment, and jumped up in excitement. "Oh yes please!" he

exclaimed excitedly. "That would be great. Can we go right now?"

"Hey slow down a bit Ben," laughed Doofus. "Aren't you a bit hungry?"

As he said that, Ben could feel his tummy rumbling. When was the last

time he had eaten anyway? He really couldn't remember. "Well maybe,"

he agreed. "That would be nice."

Tavi stood and shook herself. "Right," she said. "I'll go and get some

pancakes and bring you some of my own homemade jam to go with

them too. How does that sound?" she asked, cocking her head to one

side in an endearing way. Ben smiled. She really was an unbelievably

cute little dog, he thought. He was glad they were now friends. He

looked again at her, remembering her question. "Do you mean you cook

and things too?" he asked incredulously. Tavi and Doofus both laughed.

"Not only does she cook, and do lots more things, as you put it Ben,"

said Doofus, "but she has also won the best jam maker award for the

past three years running. Our Tavi is a proper champion." Tavi tried to

look modest, but failed, making them all laugh. "I love pancakes, and I would love to try your jam too. Thank you," said Ben. Tavi gave a little bow of appreciation and trotted out of the room.

"Apologies for Tavi," said Doofus, as the sound of Tavi's paws scampering along the stone passage disappeared. "She's very typical of her Scottie dog breed you know. She can be a bit grumpy sometimes, but she's actually very gentle and once she's your friend, she's the most loyal and trustworthy friend you could ever have. I'm sure your grandparents' dog is pretty similar?" he asked anxiously.

"I suppose so," Ben replied a little dubiously. The Tavi in his world was okay, he thought, but he had never really paid that much attention to her. She was, quite frankly, a bit boring. She just seemed to sleep, eat, and go for walks. Doofus laughed. Ben grinned sheepishly as he again remembered that Doofus could read his thoughts. "You might feel a bit different about her if she could talk to you like this Tavi eh?" grinned Doofus. "Oh yes," giggled Ben, picturing the scene and his grandparent's reactions if that happened. "Maybe next time you'll give her a bit more attention when you remember our Tavi," Doofus advised. "They are pretty similar in lots more ways than you realise you know."

Ben nodded. He wished both Tavis could talk though. That would be so much more fun.

"Tavi and I will be fine, honestly, Doofus," reassured Ben quickly. "I think both of us got a bit of a shock at the start, but I think we will be proper friends now." Doofus, who had been looking quite intensely at Ben, visibly relaxed and grinned in obvious relief. "That's great to hear," he said. "I've got some work to do, and with Dod still away at the hairdresser, I was hoping it would be okay to leave you with Tavi for a while once she returns with your pancakes. She will take you on your castle tour. Is that okay with you?"

"Of course," said Ben, who was just as keen to find out more about his new friend. He grinned broadly at the very thought.

As if she had heard (which she hadn't), Tavi returned at that moment. She was pulling a trolley proudly along behind her. The trolley was laden with a pile of something hidden under a tea towel that had a picture of a Scottie dog on it. After pushing the door closed behind her with her nose, Tavi pulled the trolley in front of Ben. She had a harness around her which was attached to the trolley. Once she was satisfied with the trolley's position she uttered, almost under her breath, "release," and the harness magically disappeared. Ben gasped with surprise. Tavi giggled. "I thought you would be impressed by that," she said. "And now, even more impressively…" Tavi waved her paw and the cloth covering the pile on the trolley was whisked off to reveal a tray with a bottle of something, Ben wasn't sure what, two glasses and a huge plate of what looked like pancakes covered by…Ben leant forward and took a double take and stared open mouthed at Tavi. He just could not quite believe his eyes. "That's tartan!" he exclaimed. "Yes," said Tavi, trying hard not to look smug and failing dismally. "It's one of my best recipes and no one else can make tartan jam quite like me. This one is the Alexander tartan, which I hope you will especially enjoy as it has family links to you, but I have lots of other tartan jam varieties too."

Ben was certainly impressed. He had never seen anything like it. "How do you manage to get it so like tartan and.." he leaned back and sighed, "it smells so delicious." Tavi and Doofus laughed, clearly delighted at Ben's reaction.

Doofus, still giggling, shuffled to the door. "I shall leave you two to enjoy yourselves for a while. Enjoy your pancakes, Ben."

Ben barely noticed Doofus's departure, so intent was he on the tasty array in front of him. He looked eagerly at Tavi. "May I?" he politely asked, fleetingly thinking his Mum would be proud of him for remembering his manners with all this excitement going on around him. "Of course – help yourself," responded Tavi, who was eagerly awaiting the delighted reaction that she was confident would happen as he tasted her prize-winning food.

of Ben and Ben needed no further encouragement. Manners now forgotten, he lifted a pancake and took a huge bite. "Oh wow…. oh WOW." He spluttered, sending crumbs flying from his

mouth. It was sensational. The pancake tasted creamy and chocolaty. Delicious! But the tartan jam was more than incredible. He could taste raspberries, strawberries…was that grapes as well….and other amazing tastes that he couldn't even begin to identify. The different tastes all seemed to pop on his tongue in separate pulsating waves. He had never, ever experienced a taste quite so wonderful before. It wasn't just a taste; it was a total immersive experience.

Ben ate five, one after another, barely aware of what he was doing, before he paused, took a deep breath and sighed the most satisfied sigh he could ever remember sighing.

"You like?" prompted Tavi smugly, broadly grinning at Ben. "That is the best thing I have ever, ever eaten." replied Ben firmly. "How did you do that?"

"My grandfather's recipe," said Tavi proudly. "Obviously, being a Scottie, we have particular expertise with every kind of Scottish food, but this tartan jam took a long time to master properly and I'm so chuffed that you like it. Does the Tavi in your world cook?" Ben giggled at the thought. "No, she doesn't. She really is nothing like you at all you know."

Tavi sighed in disappointment. "Yes, I know," she said. "Doofus and Dod have said that and tried to explain bits about your world to me lots of times, but it's so hard to believe and I feel so much for dogs in your world." She looked so sad and crestfallen, that Ben knelt on the floor beside her and gave her a hug. She gave him a quick face lick in thanks and then nudged him back to the trolley. "Have a quick drink," she said, clearly glad to change the subject. "I think you'll like our rainbow juice, and then we'll get on with our castle tour."

Ben was thirsty. He poured himself a glass and was delighted to see different rainbow colours swirling separately around in the liquid as it flowed into his glass. He took a big gulp, already knowing that this was going to taste delicious too. It didn't disappoint. This time he sensed different and completely unfamiliar tastes which swirled around his mouth, but in a much more subtle fashion than the fantastic popping of the tartan jam. He put the empty glass down and felt that he had eaten and drank his fill. His tummy felt like it had had the best feast ever. He reached down and stroked Tavi. "Thank you," he said. "That was incredible. I've never eaten or drunk anything so wonderful as that before." Tavi gave a little woof, clearly delighted. "Right, that's great," she said. "Now let's see if you enjoy our castle tour too."

Ben rose to his feet and brushed the few remaining crumbs from his clothes. Weird, he suddenly thought. When I left my bedroom I had bare feet and yet here I am with new and cosy slippers on! They fitted perfectly, and he giggled. "Yes," said Tavi with a big grin as she noticed Ben looking at his feet. "They just had to be tartan slippers didn't they." They both laughed. "Doofus popped them on your feet when you were sleeping as he was worried that you might get cold. Now," she said walking towards the door. "Are you ready?"

"Am I ever," replied Ben enthusiastically.

Chapter 6, The Castle Tour

As they walked along the corridor, Ben eagerly looked out of the window. He was, it must be said, a bit disappointed at what he saw outside. "It looks just like my world." he said dejectedly. He peered out to try to see more, but all he could see was some tall trees and a misty dullness all around. Even worse, it was pouring with rain. Tavi laughed. "That's because it is your world."

Ben stopped in his tracks and looked at her. "What do you mean, it is my world?" Tavi sighed. This was going to be difficult to explain. "We are in a different world here in the castle, but this castle is still in your world." Ben looked blankly back at Tavi. "I don't understand." Tavi tried again. "I'm not sure I understand it all either," she said. "You probably need to ask Dod more about it when you next see her, as she's much more expert on the science of this than I am." She paused, took a deep breath, thought hard and tried again. "I think it's a bit like a time warp. We are IN your world, but also BESIDE your world at the same time. We are separate, but part of you too. If it's raining in Scotland, where you live, then it's raining in Scotland too here, where we live." She looked at Ben. "Does that help?"

"Not really," said Ben. "Does that mean this castle is in my world too?"

"It is," confirmed Tavi, "but, as you can see, we've made it quite different inside to meet all our needs. We can see inside your houses, and some of us, like Doofus, can even see inside your minds,"

"But people in my world don't know you exist, and we can't see anything of your world at all," finished Ben. "Exactly," said Tavi. "Now that's clear, let's get on with our tour." It was still far from clear to Ben, but he nodded anyway, and they continued walking.

"I'm going to introduce you to a couple of my friends here first. They're very excited to meet you. You're the first human person they've actually got to see in person," Tavi laughed. "Hey, get it?" she said, "That's a good joke. Got to see in person. get it?" Ben looked blankly at her. "Oh, never mind," she said a little grumpily. "Humour is wasted on the young obviously."

At that, they opened the door into what was clearly the castle's kitchen. But it wasn't like any kitchen Ben had ever seen before. It was huge, but that wasn't what he first noticed. All around the high stone walls there were different sizes and shapes of what looked like floating shelves and tables. The shelves all seemed to be piled high. Many had books on them. As he looked around, Ben thought he had never seen so many books in one room before. It looked like there were even more than he had ever seen in Fortrose's library back at home. The books were in all sorts of random piles on the shelves and some of the piles looked like they could topple over at any time. Tavi was watching Ben and saw that he had spotted the books. "That's all my cookery books," she said proudly. "Most of them have been in my family for years, but I've also got books from other dog families around the world AND," she continued, pointing grandly to a small shelf, hanging on its own, just beside the window, "I've even got a few written by some apparently famous cooks from your world, but they're a bit disappointing I have to say." Ben nodded vaguely but was still trying to take in all that he could see around him.

There were some floating tables with nothing on them, but many of the tables had bits of food, and different crockery and cooking utensils or what looked like food mixers on them, as if someone was in the middle of preparing a meal or doing baking at the tables. On the floor of the kitchen there were more of the kitchen furniture that he was used to in his kitchen back home, only on a much grander scale. There were two big sinks, one clearly full of hot soapy water. Beside the sinks there was a huge kitchen range that had several interesting saucepans on the top, giving out delicious smells that he had never smelt before. There was what looked like a big oven underneath the range, from which more delicious smells emanated.

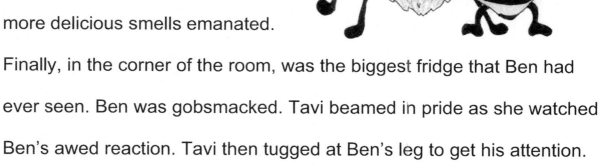

Finally, in the corner of the room, was the biggest fridge that Ben had ever seen. Ben was gobsmacked. Tavi beamed in pride as she watched Ben's awed reaction. Tavi then tugged at Ben's leg to get his attention. "Now," she said, "Meet my friends," She pulled him round and standing behind him were two creatures. One looked like a giant hairy spider, holding a mixing bowl in two of its hands (or were they legs, Ben fleetingly thought). The spider was covered in flour and had a tall, bright pink chef's hat placed at a jaunty angle on top of its head. Ben's startled eyes passed to the second creature. This one looked like a giant bee, but Ben had never seen a bee with such an enormous handlebar moustache on its face before. It too, had a chef's hat on its head, only

this one's hat was black and yellow, matching the stripes on its rather tubby body. It had an enormous spoon in one hand, and looked distracted, as it kept glancing back at the pans on the kitchen range. "Parrr...don me," it suddenly said, in an exaggerated French accent, making Ben giggle. "My sauce, it will burn if I don't…" and it flew off back to the range, buzzing in clear agitation.

Tavi sighed. "Please excuse Wahzo," she said. "His cooking means everything to him. We'll meet him properly later hopefully." Ben was trying to pronounce the bee's name the way Tavi had said it. It sounded so French-like he thought, as he repeated it inside his head silently. Ben's Auntie and Uncle lived in Switzerland and he'd heard them speaking French often and he had always enjoyed trying to speak in a French way too.

"What about me? What about me?" Ben startled back to the scene in front of him. The giant spider was waving its many limbs about, desperately trying to get his attention. It pushed forward, closer to him and Ben stepped quickly back. It did look a little scary. Tavi stepped forward between Ben and the spider. "Calm down Gugsey. Can't you see you're scaring him," she said sternly. "Remember he's never seen anything like you before, and some people, where Ben comes from are nervous of spiders." Tavi turned quickly to Ben. "Oh, and bees too, I believe. Are you okay Ben?" she said anxiously. Gugsey, the spider looked devastated and stepped back straight away.

"I'm fine, really," Ben was quick to reassure. He was actually thinking that no-one could possibly be scared of any creatures that had chef's hats on their heads and looked, well…so amazing! "My Granpa keeps bees actually, and I go to visit them sometimes." He couldn't think of anything similarly reassuring to say about spiders, but that didn't seem to matter to Gugsey, who was now beaming and… Ben peered closer to see clearer…was she? Yes, she was fluttering what looked like long eyelashes at him too. "Stop doing that fluttering thing with your eyes. It's really annoying and distracting." said Tavi sharply. "Behave yourself Gugsey". Ben had never thought that a spider could look embarrassed, but he could see that this one now did. "I'm sorry," she said. I'm just so excited to be speaking to a real person like you, I just forgot my manners." Ben smiled a little nervously. He wasn't quite sure what to make of this creature as yet. Tavi was clearly about to launch into a further ticking off for poor Gugsey, now appearing to cringe in utter embarrassment, when she was interrupted by the sudden arrival of Dod.

"Oh here you are. I've been looking everywhere. I was getting really worried. What do you mean by disappearing with him Tavi? You should know better. It might not be …" She was quickly interrupted by Tavi, who ran and jumped up at her. "It's okay Dod. It's okay honestly. Doofus said we could do a wee tour and I wasn't going to take him anywhere…" she lowered her voice suddenly, but Ben still heard her whisper "…that wasn't safe." At Dod's arrival, Gugsey had quickly scuttled off and Ben could see both she and Wahzo, the bee, furtively looking over as they busily stirred the contents of the many saucepans on the range. Dod ignored them both. "That's as maybe," she said. "Well, good to see you kept him safe, but we need to head back and get on with things. He's been away from his home for quite long enough already." Ben felt his heart sink. He didn't want to go home yet. He was having such fun. "But what about my farts," he asked anxiously. "You promised to sort them out for me." Dod, who had started to trot towards the kitchen door, turned sharply at this. "Have you had any more troubles with the farts then?" she asked rather sharply. Ben noticed, with some alarm, that Dod's horn was starting to flush with stronger pulses of rainbow colours. "Well no," replied Ben. In truth, he had forgotten all about them in the

57

excitement of everything and hadn't felt even the slightest wee bit of a fart bubble since he had woken up in the castle. However, Dod's clear concern worried him. Was there something about the farts that he should be scared of? Why did she seem so worried about him being safe? Suddenly the thought of being at home did seem like it could be a good idea. He looked down at Tavi and then back at Dod, feeling a wave of anxiety rise in his tummy. Suddenly he felt Tavi's cold wet nose touching his hand. He looked down and she smiled reassuringly at him. She had sensed his anxiety. "It will all be fine Ben, honestly," she said. She turned back and waved to Gugsey and Wahzo, who immediately waved back and also smiled and danced a funny wee jig, clearly trying to make Ben laugh. Ben couldn't help but giggle at the comical pair. "Lovely to meet you both," he said. "I'm sorry I didn't get much chance to talk more with you both."

"No worries," replied Gugsey. "We'll talk more next time. Oops…" she said as she then spotted Dod glaring at her. "Next time?" questioned Ben, looking searchingly at Dod. Dod avoided his gaze and trotted out the kitchen door. "Come on, hurry up," she called impatiently. "It's time to get those farts sorted." There was more to this than he was being told

thought Ben as he and Tavi followed her along the corridor.

Chapter 7, Preparing to Sort the Farts

This time they didn't head back to the room they had been in previously.

They turned and walked in the other direction towards a huge and very

grand staircase, which was lined with lots of different plants bearing colourful flowers, all the way up one of the sides of the staircase. Above them, in the Hall, hung a beautiful and enormous chandelier. Ben was no expert on such things, but he reckoned this must be the grandest chandelier that there ever was. It glittered and shimmered as its many hanging glass crystals reflected the light from the Hall lamps.

The Hall floor was, Ben supposed, wooden as were the stairs and the bannister, but the wood felt so smooth and it shone. Someone must have spent a lot of time polishing this floor he thought.

The walls too, were panelled with wood, and they had strange paintings in very fancy frames hung on them. Ben tried to look closer as they walked by. They looked vaguely like the portraits he had seen in some of the old castles he had visited with Mum and Dad back at home, but these portraits were unlike anything he had ever seen before. They were all paintings of different, but very posh looking, creatures. He recognised a dragon, not unlike Doofus, in one of them, but there were some others that he wasn't even sure what kind of creatures they were paintings of. He thought fleetingly of his Granny, who loved to paint. She would love to see these he was sure.

His eye was suddenly caught by one particular painting. There were three smiling children depicted in it. A little girl with dark curly hair, who looked straight out towards him with a look of defiance, whilst tightly clutching a huge book. The second figure was a bigger girl with fair hair who seemed to have a glowing golden foot. He couldn't see her face clearly as her face was turned slightly away as she gazed up at the last figure. It was this last figure that really caught his attention though. As he looked closer, he saw that it was a boy, perhaps a teenager, thought Ben, but he saw such a strong resemblance to himself. It was spooky and somehow made him shiver. He would have liked to have stopped to spend a bit more time looking at the paintings, but he then saw Doofus waiting for them at the bottom of the stairs, so he hurried over to join him, along with Dod and Tavi.

"I've got the bathroom all ready for you," said Doofus smiling at Ben. Doofus then looked over to Dod. "Oh," he said. "Nice hair cut Dod. You look lovely." Dod was clearly delighted at this and tossed her mane dramatically to show it off better. Ben waited for the golden dust to fall, but nothing happened. A bit disappointed, he tried to smile at Dod in an admiring sort of way. He felt a bit bad. He hadn't even noticed that she'd

had her hair cut. Doofus smothered a giggle and winked at Ben.

Dod seemed calmer again now, after her clear irritation when finding

them in the kitchen. Her horn had reassuringly returned back to its

normal hue. She stopped and turned to Ben and Tavi. "You had better

say goodbye to each other just now," she said. She smiled at Tavi. "I

know how much you hate baths Tavi, and we need to take Ben for his

bath now I'm afraid." Tavi visibly shuddered at the mere mention of a

bath. It was apparent that dogs here hated baths as much as dogs in

Ben's world did.

"But…," started Ben. He really didn't want to leave Tavi yet. There was

so much more he wanted to see, do and find out with his new friend. "No

buts Ben," Dod said firmly. "We've already waited much longer than we

should have."

Tavi pushed her nose again into Ben's hand. "It's for the best," she tried

to say reassuringly, but Ben could see that she was upset too. Then she

looked up at him and gave a secret little wink that Ben was sure she was

hiding from Dod. "I think this is au revoir, but not goodbye, if you know what I mean?" she whispered. She winked again, gave his hand a little lick and scampered off down the corridor. Ben wasn't quite sure what Tavi had been trying to say to him, though he knew that au revoir was French for goodbye. There was something that he was missing here – yet again. He tried to fight the tears suddenly beginning to prick at his eyes and the huge lump that had suddenly appeared in his throat. Swallowing hard, he turned back from watching Tavi and looked at Dod and Doofus.

Doofus shuffled over and patted his shoulder sympathetically. He, of course, was well aware of how upset Ben was at saying goodbye to Tavi. "I know it's hard Ben, but it will feel better soon, you'll see," he said. Then, he too, mysteriously winked at Ben. Weirder and weirder thought Ben. However, he got no further chance to think about it all, as Dod, with much tutting and mane shaking, urged him to hurry up the stairs. Reluctantly Ben obediently followed her, as Doofus lumbered up the stairs behind them both.

Upstairs seemed smaller than downstairs. Well, at least the corridor was narrower. Dod hurried Ben past several closed doors, until they reached the open door of what was obviously a bathroom. Ben gasped and stopped abruptly in the doorway. This was a bathroom unlike any he had ever seen before. Like all the other rooms that Ben had seen in the castle, it was huge. He looked up, distracted initially by the sound of rain (yes, it was still raining!), hammering down on the huge glass domed roof that stretched across the room above him. "It's a shame it's raining so heavily," said Doofus, as he followed Ben's gaze. "It's really quite beautiful in here on a lovely day, and even nicer at night when you can see all the stars." Ben nodded and continued to stare open mouthed as he tried to take in all he saw within the room. Taking precedence in the centre of the room was the bath, but it was more like a mini swimming pool than a bath Ben thought. It had sloping, roll topped tile mosaic sides. The same mosaics covered the base of the bath and he was mesmerised by the images the tiles portrayed. They looked like lots of exotic looking fish that seemed to ripple and move, making the water move and even splash in places, as if the fish were alive, although he could see they were just pictures and not real fish at all. The colours were beautiful.

Tearing his eyes away from the bath, Ben looked over to one side of the room where he saw not just one, but three toilets. Each toilet was separated from each other by tiled partitions, though he couldn't see any doors to close them off for privacy. The toilets were all different sizes. The first one was of similar size to the toilets that he was used to back home. The second one was of in-between size and the third was about three times the size of the first one. It was enormous! Each toilet had a matching hand basin beside it. The basins were shaped to look like different kinds of flowers, and all were in beautiful colours. Doofus giggled as he watched Ben. "There needs to be the different sizes of toilets you know, because we are all different sizes and shapes too."

Doofus pointed to the smallest toilet. "I couldn't really fit into that cubicle, now could I?" Ben laughed delightedly. This was definitely the best room he had yet seen. The toilets were brilliant! Who could ever have thought that toilets could be so amazing? The details were fantastic. Even the flush handles on each toilet were special. They were all designed to look like birds. The smallest toilet's handle looked like a robin, the middle one was a duck and the biggest was a magnificent swan.

Dod gave one of her signature "harrumphs" and again shook her mane in obvious impatience. "I know it's all great fun boys," she said a little testily, "but time is getting on." She began to tap her hoof testily on the floor, clearly irritated at what she saw as time wasting.

Doofus sighed and frowned at Dod. "I know you're right Dod," he said, "but it's so much fun watching and listening to Ben's reactions to all of this. It's like seeing our home for the first time again. Surely we don't have to rush him quite so much…?"

Dod paused and looked at Ben. She, in turn, sighed. It seemed so long ago since she was his age and a young unicorn foal. A flash of memory reminded her of a young foal giggling and prancing with delight as she had done when she had first arrived at the castle and seen all its magical rooms too. She took a deep breath and consciously made herself calm down and she tried to push her anxiousness away. Now smiling properly at them both, she nodded at Doofus. "He will get a chance to sit and play in the bath for a while, I promise, but" she continued, "we need to explain things to him first. You know how important this all is Doofus."

Doofus nodded and turned back to Ben, who was slowly wandering around the room in complete fascination with all he could see. He kept looking longingly at the bath. There was steam gently rising from it and, when he dipped his hands in the water, it felt silky and warm as it flowed through his fingers.

"We have a lot to tell you Ben. Perhaps it might be more fun though for you to sit and enjoy a relaxing bath whilst we try to explain everything to you? We can get rid of your troublesome farts too once we've had a chat?" Ben had completely forgotten about his farts. He now remembered that he had been told that a bath was needed to get rid of the farts. He looked anxiously at the water. Suddenly it didn't seem such a good attraction anymore.

Dod saw his face. "Don't worry Ben. Nothing bad is going to happen to you, I promise! We will first explain quickly how the farts will be sorted, then get rid of them and neither of these will take very long and it will probably make you laugh. Then, afterwards, you can choose whether you want to stay in the bath, or come out and sit with us, whilst we explain about getting you back home and afterwards...." Her words tailed off and she again looked at Doofus anxiously. Unnoticed by Ben, Doofus moved quickly to Dod's side and stroked her mane in a caring and reassuring way.

Ben was thinking hard. He swallowed several times and looked defiantly at them both. "I'm not moving or going anywhere," he said firmly, "until you do both stop hiding things from me and explain what's going on properly. You've both been hiding things from me ever since I got here. I'm not a baby you know." He stood up and stamped his foot. "I'm not afraid," he said defiantly, though he did feel butterflies in his tummy that were making him feel not quite so brave as he was trying to show.

Both Doofus and Dod looked a bit startled, and then Doofus raised his head and gave such a loud guffaw of laughter. "We should have realised Ben," he said, looking proudly down at him. He grinned at Dod. "The magic didn't choose Ben by accident Dod" he said. "Just look at him.

He's a real hero, you know." Ben was stunned. "What do you mean?" he asked. "How am I a hero?"

"Because, young man, you have so far taken everything in your stride. You've accepted it all, stayed calm, made friends, and now, even when you don't know what's going on, you are showing how brave and sensible you can be." Doofus turned to Dod. "I think we have been misjudging the abilities and strength of Ben, Dod. The magic knew exactly what it was doing when it entered Ben's fart centre. It knew that Ben was the one to help us all."

Dod looked searchingly at Ben and smiled broadly. "You are right Doofus," she confirmed. "How did we not realise this earlier." Ben didn't know what to think. So many thoughts were now whizzing around in his head. He was certainly confused, but also proud that they could think so highly of him and his anxious tummy butterflies had returned. What did all this mean? He swallowed hard. "I think I really need to know what this all about don't I?" he asked as he gave a slightly nervous smile.

"You're right Ben." said Doofus, returning a sympathetic smile. He shuffled across to a cupboard door, that had been cleverly disguised, so that it wasn't obvious within the leafy wallpaper that lined the walls. He dragged a large furry red rug from the cupboard and laid in on the wooden floor in front of Ben. Squatting down on the rug, Doofus encouraged both Dod and Ben to settle down beside him. "We might as well be comfortable," he said. "There's a lot of explaining to do." He looked at Dod and waited expectantly.

"Okay,okay. You are right Doofus," said Dod. She flashed him a grin, before continuing, "As usual actually." Ben felt that his tummy was now doing somersaults. His nervousness returned and he felt like things were all getting a bit too crazy all of a sudden. He wasn't sure that he did really want to hear any explanations after all. He closed his eyes and tried to think of his cosy bedroom back home. Maybe this was all just a dream, he thought. Maybe if he closed his eyes long enough, then he would just wake up back in his own bed. He felt a gentle touch on his hand and opened his eyes and looked down at his hand. Doofus's giant paw was gently stroking his hand. "Hang on in there Ben," he said. "I know so much has happened, and I know you are feeling a bit scared and a bit out of control, but it is going to get better and…," Ben felt Doofus squeezing his hand and he looked up into Doofus's face to see such care and concern mirrored there. "And," continued Doofus softly, as he held Ben's gaze, "I promise with everything I hold dear, that Dod and I would never, ever let anything bad happen to you." Dod nodded vigorously in agreement, causing some golden dust to settle glitteringly on the rug beside them. She frowned and Ben knew she was thinking about the mess the dust was making. It made him smile. "That's better," said Dod, clearly relieved. And she began to talk.

Chapter 8, Explanations at Last

"I spoke a bit about the magic to you earlier when we were in your bedroom, do you remember Ben?" said Dod.

"Yes," he said. "You said that you thought some young magic had got into me when I paddled in the sea and that it shouldn't have left your world, but that it was maybe being misch…mischev…" he stumbled. "Mischievous," finished Dod with a smile. "That's right, well done. We now think that maybe it wasn't being mischievous at all. We think it entered you on purpose."

"But WHY and why me?" interrupted Ben impatiently. It all sounded so unlikely to him. Dod sighed. "I'm trying to explain Ben. Please try to be patient." Doofus again squeezed Ben's hand and smiled encouragingly at him. Ben muttered an apology and tried to settle himself again. Dod waited a minute until Ben stopped squirming, then continued. "We think the magic knew that once we found out about your troublesome farts that we would come to help you and that once we got to know you, then we would realise how special you are!" She paused and smiled. "Just as we now have, though maybe a bit more slowly than we should have." Ben flushed red in embarrassment and pride, even though he wasn't really sure why he should feel that way either.

"Why couldn't the magic just come and get you to do what it wanted itself? Why does it need me anyway? Surely magic can just magic things better itself?" Ben demanded. He opened his mouth, about to ask more, but stopped when he saw Dod's face. She looked stern again. "I'm sorry," he muttered. "I'll try not to interrupt again." Dod began again. "I will try to answer your last questions, as hopefully that will help you begin to see, and…" she glared at Ben, "stop you interrupting!"

Doofus laughed, and Ben smiled gratefully at him.

"The magic isn't like people, or even Doofus and me, Ben." Said Dod. "It doesn't have a body. There is nothing that you can see or feel. It is just in the air around us, but it can enter people and all sort of other things too, like the cocoa plants and even like the tables in the kitchen downstairs." Ben smiled at the memory of the floating tables with all their funny piles on top of them. "The magic's main purpose is to to change things to try to make things better for your world and ours," she continued. "There is still a lot of things about magic that have yet to understand though. We know that's it's much stronger and more obvious in our world than it is in your world, but it does have the same purpose in both worlds. We also know that there are lots of different magic, erm…," she paused trying to find the right word, "…sort of pieces, I suppose. Each of these pieces seem to grow, like we do, from being very young pieces, to fully mature and adult-like pieces. These pieces can do their magic individually, like the piece that's in your fart centre, or they can join together to do bigger and stronger magic, like making Doofus and I."

"Wh..at…?" gasped Ben in astonishment. "You are both made by magic? Are you properly alive and real then?" Ben didn't know what to make of this startling news. Doofus and Dod both laughed. "We are both very much alive and real Ben." The magic made us a long time ago, to help them to sort out some things that they couldn't manage to sort with their magic alone. They use us for lots of things like helping to explain things, in both worlds, and for finding out things that they need answers to themselves. Sometimes the magic makes mistakes, just like people do, and we also help to fix these mistakes."

Ben had a sudden unhappy thought. "I'm not a mistake, am I?" he said in a small voice. "Of course not," replied Doofus, reaching to squeeze Ben's hand again. "We did think at first, as you know, that the magic entering your fart centre might have been a mistake, but you are very special Ben. You are certainly NOT a mistake. You are so special that you might even be someone who could help magic in very important ways more in the future," he stated proudly. "Not now, Doofus," snapped Dod a little sharply. "That's something to talk about later with Ben's Mum and Dad, not for now." Ben looked shocked and wanted to ask more but was silenced by a stern look from Dod and a rather sheepish, but firm shake of the head from Doofus. He sighed. Sometimes being seen as a child all the time just wasn't fair. It didn't seem right that he had to wait for grownups to decide what was good for him to know all the time, rather than being able to decide for himself. Doofus stifled a giggle beside him and tried to look sternly at Ben, but couldn't help himself giving Ben a knowing wink, which he tried to hide from Dod. Dod did notice the wink, but chose to ignore it.

"I think that's enough big explanations for now Ben. I think it's now time to get those troublesome farts sorted for you."

"But you just said that the magic entered my fart centre on purpose?" he said with a giggle. The whole fart centre thing still sounded so silly and ridiculous to him. He really wanted to know more about that too, but, seeing Dod's face, he rightly thought it wiser not to interrupt further.

"The magic did enter on purpose," confirmed Dod, "so that we would come to help you, but that doesn't alter the fact that the magic doesn't belong there and your farts will continue to give you increasing amounts of trouble until we help the magic out from your fart centre. It's stuck there at the moment. It's been quiet since you arrived here because it sensed that it's closer to its magical home, but, for all its clever, it doesn't know how to escape. If it's left there it will get more annoyed and make your farts even more troublesome. Magic isn't always blessed with a lot of patience you know."

"Oh," said Ben. There really wasn't any answer to an explanation like that. "What do I need to do then?" He looked anew at the bath. "You said that having a bath would get rid of it?"

Pleased to see that Ben was reacting so well, Dod beamed at him. "Thanks Ben. You are a star. Yes, a bath will sort it out, and so quickly and easily too."

"How," asked Ben bluntly. "It won't hurt will it?" he told himself he would be brave if he had to be, but he would really rather he didn't have to be.

"It won't hurt at all," reassured Doofus quickly. "In fact, you might find it funny and maybe a bit tickly, that's all." Ben considered a moment. That didn't so bad then after all. "Right," he said, standing up quickly. "Let's get on with it."

Doofus and Dod both laughed and looked relieved.

"Thanks Ben. Right, all you need to do is to slip out of your clothes, as you won't want to head home in wet clothes, and then just pop yourself into the bath." She turned to Doofus. "Have you got the collection tube ready?" she asked him. Doofus pulled out a clear glass tube with a stopper at its top from his tummy pouch. "Ready," he confirmed.

Ben looked at the tube, his mind racing. What was Doofus planning to do with that?"

Doofus gave out a great bellow of laughter as he saw Ben's face. He struggled to find his words as he continued to giggle. Ben's growing indignation at Doofus's obvious amusement, only made Doofus laugh even more. After a minute or two, now facing indignation from Dod too, Doofus managed to get himself back under some control. "I'm so….rry…" he struggled to say. He swallowed. "I'm sorry Ben. It was just your face…...!" Realising that he was about to start giggling again, he turned to Dod. "You explain Dod please?" he asked a little breathlessly. Glaring in disgust at Doofus, she did.

"When you are in the bath at home Ben, do you ever notice that farts seem to come out more easily when you are under water?" Ben nodded, trying not to giggle himself now. "And what happens then to the farts when they come out under water?" she asked.

"They come up in bubbles and pop on the surface," Ben replied. He looked at the glass tube and understanding dawned on him. "Oh I see," he said, now grinning at Doofus. "You are going to collect what's inside the bubbles in that tube."

"Correct." Said Dod. "Well done. The warm water makes your fart centre relax and the magic can more easily escape then. The water in this bath also has some added magic essence, which will help even more."

Ben quickly undressed and excitedly hopped into the bath. It felt so good. The water felt silky and smooth against his skin, He loved it, but what was even better was the reaction of the fish patterns on the mosaic. Although he could see that they were just drawings, they actually moved! Initially, they swam out of his way and went to the other side of the large bath away from him, but after a few seconds they seemed to gain confidence and they swam back over to him and nibbled his toes and fingers. He giggled as the nibbles and the water flow around him both tickled. The fish began to splash a little. They seemed to be having fun too.

"Ok fellows," said Doofus, leaning over the bath and speaking directly to the fish. "You've met him, but now off you go so that we can get on with what we need to do." The fish swam dutifully over to the other side of the bath. "Now," said Doofus. "I want you to take a deep breath and hold

onto it for a second, and then imagine that you are trying to blow up a balloon with your bottom." Ben giggled but did as he was told. They all waited expectantly. They didn't have to wait long. Ben started to giggle in earnest. It felt so tickly. Then Whoosh! The bubbles burst out of Ben's bottom and Doofus deftly unstoppered the glass tube and caught the

81

bubbles as they rose to the surface. He then quickly replaced the stopper.

Ben looked eagerly at the tube and then slumped down back into the bath. "There's nothing to see," he said in disappointment. "Not much, no," agreed Dod, "But if you look closer you might see a bit of a golden glow shining out." Ben looked closer and Yes; he could just make it a shimmer of gold.

"Hello and goodbye magic," he said softly to the glow. "Thank you for giving me such an adventure." Dod and Doofus looked at each other and smiled. Ben was indeed a special boy.

"What will happen to the magic now," asked Ben, as he watched the glow wobble about inside the collection tube. "It won't get into trouble will it?" He felt protective and somehow still connected to the magic. It had, after all, been inside him for some time.

Doofus laughed. "No, it won't," he replied. "We will take it somewhere quiet and let it rest and recover for a little while. We need to check that it's okay after it's adventure, and then it will be released. It will be fine," he reassured. Ben, now distracted by the playful fish around him in the bath, nodded happily at this. He barely noticed Doofus leave the room

with the tube, returning just a few minutes later empty handed.

Chapter 9, Returning Home

Ben was reluctant to get out of the bath. He would have liked to have stayed to play longer with the fish, who were still happily swimming and splashing about beside him, but he eventually obeyed the urgings of Dod, and was then quick to get himself dried and back into his clothes.

"So that's it," he said sadly. "That's my adventure over and I have to go home again now I suppose." He slowly followed Dod and Doofus out of the bathroom, dragging his feet tiredly as he plodded on behind them. Doofus stopped and turned back to Ben. "Well, we do need to get you back home indeed, but I'm not sure that that will be the end of your adventures Ben, you know."

"What do you mean?" said Ben, startled. He rushed over to Doofus, trying to read the expression on Doofus's face. He was worried that Doofus was just teasing him. Doofus laughed. "No joke Ben," he reassured him. "Come and have a look at this." Ben's mind was racing as he followed along behind Doofus. Once again, he felt like there was so much happening around him that he couldn't get a grasp of. It all felt overwhelming. He was excited again, but also a little scared. He also realised that he was missing his family and his own home again. Suddenly, he realised he was really, really tired. Without realising what he was doing, he slowed right down again. Doofus, of course, responded immediately. Without saying a word, he returned back to Ben and gently nudged him helpfully a few steps further along the corridor. He stopped Ben there and turned him towards the wall.

"Now look at this please Ben." Doofus said gently. Wearily Ben lifted his head and found himself staring at the painting of the three children he had noticed earlier. "What do you think?" asked Doofus, as he closely watched Ben, looking to see his reaction. "I saw this earlier," replied Ben, still feeling too tired to really pay attention. "I thought the boy looked a bit like me."

"That's because it IS you." replied Doofus. All thoughts of tiredness momentarily disappeared. Ben stared in amazement at Doofus. "What do you mean? It can't be." Ben said. He started to feel a bit cross. This was just silliness surely. "It really IS you, Ben," said Doofus, "but it's you in the future. You have a younger sister, don't you?" Doofus pointed at the fair-haired girl, who was looking up at the boy in the painting. "Don't you think she looks a bit like this girl too?"

Ben peered closely at the painting again. Now as Doofus said that, Ben could see a similarity and his Carys did have a missing foot that could maybe explain the golden glow on one of her lower legs as a fancy artificial foot. "But," Ben said, still not believing Doofus. "I don't have another sister, so who's that?" He said, pointing at the smaller dark haired younger girl. He glared back at Doofus, who sighed in response and shook his head. "We don't know," he admitted ruefully. "But we know this is important Ben. It's important for you obviously, but it's also very important for both of our worlds we believe. We are going to take you home now and speak to your parents to see if they can help us make sense of it all."

Ben just wasn't sure what to think. He really did want to see his family now, but he was also nervous that he might somehow get into trouble with his Mum and Dad for disappearing without them knowing. Who was going to believe all of this anyway? It all sounded so unbelievable. And he was so very tired.

Ben's troubled thoughts were interrupted by the clip, clop of Dod's approaching hooves. She looked harassed and a bit distracted as she arrived. She had a large empty bag with her and directed Doofus to lift the painting down from the wall, which he quickly did. Carefully she put it into the bag, with padding around it to protect it. She then returned it to Doofus, who, with a bit of effort, managed to squeeze it gently into his tummy pouch. Ben gasped as it seemed to magically shrink as it disappeared into the pouch. "Doesn't that hurt?" he asked Doofus in concern. "Not at all," reassured Doofus with a grin.

Meantime Dod had closed her eyes and had taken several deep breaths. Now apparently calmer, she opened her eyes looked searchingly at Ben. She was shocked to see how tired he looked. "Oh Ben, I'm so sorry," she said. "Removing the farts from you will have

really tired you out, and that's on top of all the excitement and adventure of coming here too." She looked at Doofus. "We mustn't delay any longer," she said urgently. "We need to get him home now." Doofus nodded and clasped Ben's hand within his giant paw. "We will explain more and help you and your family to understand as much as we know, once we get you back home again Ben," he reassured. "We are both coming with you. Now take your slippers off and lift your jumper as you did before." Ben nodded dully and obligingly took his beautiful tartan slippers off and handed them to Doofus. He was so tired that he barely noticed Doofus as she violently shook her mane to and fro, causing a pile of golden dust to begin to gather on the wooden floor. Doofus helped him to lift up his jumper and steered Ben to stand him in the pile of golden dust. Ben was vaguely aware of Dod's glowing horn moving close to his tummy and then…. then he woke up once again in his own bedroom, safely tucked up in his own cosy bed.

So it was all a dream, he thought as he opened his eyes and focussed on his lovely Batman mural that Mum had painted on his wall beside his bed for him. He sighed. It had been the most exciting dream he had ever had though. Smiling to himself, Ben started to snuggle back down under the duvet, when he heard a muffled giggle behind him. Turning over, Ben was stunned to see Doofus and Dod sitting on the bedroom floor looking at him. Both were grinning broadly at him. "We thought you would never wake up. You've been sleeping for ages!" said Doofus.

Ben threw the duvet back and clambered out of the bed. He felt like he had been asleep for ages too. "You are real!" he shouted excitedly, as he rushed to give them both a hug. Doofus proudly passed the tartan slippers to Ben, who nodded thanks and gleefully put them back on his feet. They certainly felt very real and very cosy. He sighed. Could this really be happening to him?

He was suddenly distracted by a noise from downstairs. "Ben are you ok?" he heard his Mum shout. Feeling a bit panicked, Benn looked desperately at Doofus and Dod. What should he do? "Don't worry," said Doofus quickly. "We have arrived back here at the same time as we first left before we took you to our castle, so your Mum doesn't even realise that you've been away anywhere. But we DO now need to meet your family and explain things to you all." Ben was a bit taken aback to see Doofus look so seriously at him. He swallowed and then he began to grin. This could be really funny he suddenly thought. How would Mum and Dad react to seeing Doofus and Dod?

"Mum, can you and Dad please come upstairs right now, I've got something very, very important to show you both?" he shouted, grinning back at the encouraging smiles from Doofus and Dod. He heard Mum saying something to Dad and then listened as he heard them both muttering as they came up the stairs. Looking at Doofus and Dod, he couldn't help but giggle. Dod looked sternly at him, shaking her head,

but Doofus was clearly trying to stifle a giggle as well.

Chapter 10, The End of An Adventure – Maybe?

Ben was actually a bit disappointed by how well his parents reacted to Doofus and Dod. His Mum didn't scream, not even once, and his Dad didn't even get angry. They were certainly shocked, but, once they saw that Ben was well and happy, they were more curious than anything. However, there wasn't time for big explanations just then, as Dad had to go and collect Carys and bring her home from nursery.

Several cups of tea (or hot chocolate in both Ben and Carys's case) later, and everyone now suitably calm and accepting of the situation, they settled down around the kitchen table to properly discuss the situation. Carys, who had immediately fallen in love with Dod, refused to sit at the table, and was now cosily nestled up beside Dod as Dod half lay and half sat on the kitchen floor.

"I just think it's so funny that you both have the same names that my sister Laura and I call each other," said Mum. She had been giggling on and off almost since she had first been introduced to them. "What do you mean, the same names?" asked Dod, looking confused. "I can't quite remember how or when it first started," explained Mum, "but when we were on our own together as children and teenagers, or nowadays when we are speaking on the phone, we have always called each other Dod and Doofus. I'm Doofus and Laura is Dod."

Doofus nearly knocked his cup of tea over as he startled in shock at this revelation. "Did you hear that Dod?" he exclaimed, clearly excited. Dod too, looked shocked and shook her mane distractedly, causing Carys to giggle with delight as little bits of golden dust settled on her and tickled her. "Does your sister have any children?" asked Doofus. "Yes," replied Ben, before Mum could reply. "I have a cousin called Evie, but she's still a baby and is only just starting to walk. They live in Switzerland you know." He stopped abruptly as Doofus appeared to "Whoop," in delight. "This confirms the linkage even more you realise." Doofus almost shouted in excitement, now broadly grinning and staring at Dod.

"Hey, what about letting us in on this?" asked Dad. "This sounds important."

Making a visible attempt to calm himself down, Doofus replied. "It is important, and very significant." Seeing their clear confusion, he looked over to Dod. "You'll explain it all better than I will," he said. "I'll just get emotional and excited." Dod smiled at this but nodded in agreement. "You're probably right," she said, and she began to explain.

"We believe that your family has all the signs of an exceptional connection with magic. There is so much evidence to now support this." She looked tenderly at Carys and then smiled at Ben. "Ben was obviously the one who first brought this to our attention. He has the strongest and most natural magic connection that we have ever seen in a person before. The magic is drawn to him and it seems to know that he can help the magic too." Ben looked puzzled at this, and wanted to ask more, but was stopped by a gentle paw pat from Doofus. "There is much more though," continued Dod. "Let's start with Ben's Grandparents. Ben tells us that they have a Scottie dog called Tavi." Ben couldn't help himself, he quickly interrupted. "I've got a new friend

94

now in Magicarea, that's the name of the other world you know, "he said seeing his parents confused faces, "and she's called Tavi, and she's a Scottie dog and she TALKS!" he proudly stated. Dod and Doofus smiled indulgently at Ben's clear delight. Carys giggled, but Mum and Dad just looked in some disbelief at Dod. "It's quite true," replied Doofus, as he lifted his paw and did a high five with Ben in celebration. He was clearly about to say more, but Dod continued on. "The fact that you and your sister have been using our names," she paused and actually winked, much to both Ben and Carys's delight, "and they are such unusual names too," she added. "That is especially strong evidence in itself." Dod looked directly at Ben's Mum. "You have shown signs too, of innate magical knowledge, especially relating to your often timely use of chocolate, which has high levels of magic within it." Ben nodded at this, and was about to add more, but was gently distracted from doing so by another paw tap from Doofus. Dod turned to Ben's Dad. "Your family may have a connection too, though not as obvious as on Ben's Mum's side." Dad looked unconvinced but listened attentively as Dod continued. "Your family keeps bees I understand?" Ben interrupted again. "Yes, Grandpa does, and I've also met a funny bee called Wahzo and…"

"Later Ben," said Doofus softly. Ben sighed loudly and frowned, but he didn't continue. Why did grown ups always have to be the bosses, he thought. Dod stifled a giggle and continued. "Bees are natural nurturers and carers in our world too due to their production and skills in making honey which is, of course, often used alongside chocolate to help with magic health and wellbeing." Dod paused and looked over to Doofus. "Will you show them the painting please?" All watched in utter amazement as Doofus reached into his pouch and slowly brought forth the painting. It seemed to grow bigger and as it squeezed out of the pouch and Doofus screwed up his eyes in obvious effort as it slowly emerged. He carefully removed the painting from its protective bag and propped it up on the kitchen worktop. Everyone scrambled over to see it. Dod helped Carys up onto her back so that she could get a better view, much to Carys's clear delight. Ben felt a bit jealous of her, but Mum lifted him up too and gave him a tight squeeze of reassurance. "This is however, the most important and clear evidence we have," stated Dod grandly. As they looked, she pointed to the three figures within the painting. Mum gasped. "That's Ben," she said, "But an older Ben."

Dod nodded. "Indeed, it is," she said. "And look Carys," she said, as she leaned closer to let Carys see better. "That's you." Carys looked and giggled. "I like my hair," she said and then pointed to the golden foot that seemed to shine out from the painting. "And that prosthetic looks much better than the one I have now." She exclaimed. "Indeed, it does," said Dad a little breathlessly.

Dod pointed finally the third small figure. "We didn't understand this one though, until Ben just now told us about his cousin Evie."

"You think that's Evie?" asked Ben in some disbelief. "We most definitely do." Replied Dod firmly. "As you can see, this painting shows the three children as much older than they are just now." Dod continued to explain. "We believe that they will have another big adventure," she paused and smiled, as Ben again interrupted, but this time with an exclamation of obvious delight. "I knew it." he said, remembering Tavi's strange remarks and eye wink as they had parted. "Tavi was trying to tell

97

me that I would see her again." He raced through to the living room and back again, super charged now with excitement and glee.

Mum sighed. "I think we need a break and some calm down time before we hear more now," as she watched Ben, now followed by a giggling Carys, caper and giggle in the living room.

The break led to dinner, as they all realised how hungry they were. Doofus was fascinated by the way that Dad prepared and cooked the meal. He and Dad could be heard giggling and laughing as Dad tried to explain the many actions involved with preparing the dinner to a dragon who had never seen a person cooking before. Ben and Carys roared with laughter at some of Doofus's many questions and funny reactions to everything. He was especially fascinated by how Dad peeled the potatoes. He had never seen anyone make chips from potatoes before apparently. Ben and Carys, and even Dad too, found it all highly amusing and hard to believe.

Mum and Dod sat through in the living room whist the meal was being prepared, and Mum reminisced with Dod about her childhood days with her sister and their Mum. Dod listened with fascination and interrupted only occasionally with questions.

After dinner, which Doofus professed to be one of the best meals he had ever had, much to Dad's delight, talk again turned to the magic and the children's future as depicted in the painting.

"We have found out more about all of this since we released the magic from Ben," said Dod. "The magic that entered Ben, was we initially thought, just a very unusual young and clever piece of magic. We were wrong." Dod paused seeing the look of anxiety and concern that passed between Ben's Mum and Dad. Ben too, looked a little alarmed. This was scary news. "What was it then?" he asked nervously. "We now know that this magic was a special messenger from the magic hierarchy." Ben looked blankly at Doofus. Doofus, leant forward and whispered in Ben's ear. "I know it's confusing," he said, "but just listen just now. I'll explain it all more to you later." Ben nodded and gave a little smile in response. Dod continued again.

"The magic has apparently had some sort of a prophesy, known to the magic hierarchy for many, many years, but unknown by most magic and certainly unknown by us until now. The prophesy describes three children," Dod pointed to the painting, "as shown in this painting, who will be the salvation of both our world and of your world too, since both worlds are really the same in so many ways."

There was silence in the room as all, even Carys, tried to understand this and tried to see what the implications would be for them all. Ben's Mum and Dad looked at each other and then at Dod. "Now wait a minute…" Dad started to say in protest but was interrupted by Dod. "I know," she said. "It's unbelievable isn't it."

Ben abruptly stood up and glared at them all. "It's unbelievable that I've eaten tartan jam." He said angrily. "It's unbelievable that dogs and spiders and bees can talk. It's unbelievable that we are sitting here with a dragon and a unicorn too," he stopped and smiled a little apologetically at Doofus, before  continuing, "but all this is actually happening!" He turned once more to Doofus. "You told me I was a hero before, and I didn't believe you then.

I'm still not sure that I am a proper hero now, but I do know that it was ME…" he shouted, now visibly upset and angry …" that the magic chose and it's ME that isn't going to let them down and it's ME that is going to do my very, very best to do everything that I can to help whether you help or you don't. SO THERE!" With that, he put out his hand to Carys, who took it and also glared defiantly back at the stunned audience. Ben and Carys then marched out of the kitchen, slamming the door behind them.

After a few minutes of stunned silence, Doofus was the first to speak. "Your son IS a hero you know, and it looks like his sister is too. This is bigger than all of us, you know."

Hours later, Ben lay tucked up safely in his bed once more, cuddling the little miniature Doofus soft toy that Doofus had given him as he had said au revoir before leaving with Dod to return to Magicarea. Ben thought of Carys, now sound asleep through in her bedroom, similarly clutching a miniature toy Dod as she slept. He smiled. He and Carys, and little Evie, were going to save the world. He just knew it, and he promptly fell asleep.

A drawing of Ben dreaming.Beside him, Doofus the toy dinosaur sighed contentedly. He knew they were going to save the world too. He smiled, snuggled into the sleeping Ben and within minutes he too, was sound asleep.

THE END

About The Author

As a retired nurse, I've always tried to keep busy! Covid lockdown found me looking for more personal challenges.

Following Ben, my grandson, sadly telling me over the phone one night how much he missed me, I decided this was the time to write for him that children's book that I had always thought of – but had been too intimidated to actually try!

I loved the whole writing and illustrating experience and hope to do more featuring my other gorgeous grandchildren.

My intention is to write more books featuring each and all of my grandchildren. Who knows when time and obligations will allow this to happen.

Epilogue

Writing "Ben Alexander and His Magic Farts" has been an enjoyable experience and my intention is to write more books featuring each and all of my grandchildren.

Who knows when time and obligations will allow this to happen?

Debbie A. Smith,

Author.

Printed in Great Britain
by Amazon

66765252R10061